D0189905

Bob's Bobble Hat

by Margaret Nash

Illustrated by Tripee

Notes on the series

TIDDLERS are structured to provide support for children who are starting to read on their own. The stories may also be used for sharing with children.

Starting to read alone can be daunting. **TIDDLERS** help by listing the words in the book for a check before reading, and by providing visual support and repeating words and phrases. These books will both develop confidence and encourage reading and rereading for pleasure.

If you are reading this book with a child, here are a few suggestions:

1. Make reading fun! Choose a time to read when you and the child are relaxed and have time to share the story.
2. Talk about the story before you start reading. Look at the cover and the blurb. What might the story be about? Why might the child like it?
3. Look also at the list of words below - can the child tackle most of the words?
4. Encourage the child to retell the story, using the jumbled picture puzzle.
5. Give praise! Remember that small mistakes need not always be corrected.

Here is a list of the words in this story.

Common words:

a	hat	no
baby	have	now
can	he	off
did	is	said
dog	it	the
everyone	like	to
got	new	you

Other words:

Ann	Bob	not
bit	bobble	threw
	happy	

Bob got a new hat.

TO
BOB

3

He did not like
the bobble.

4

"You can have it,"
he said to Ann.

7

"No!" said Ann.

8

"You can have it,"
Ann said to the baby.

The baby threw the hat.

The dog got it.

The dog bit off
the bobble.

Now everyone
is happy!

Puzzle Time

Can you find these
pictures in the story?

Which pages are the
pictures from?

Turn over for answers!

Answers

The pictures come from these pages:

a. pages 12–13

b. pages 18–19

c. pages 4–5

d. pages 8–9

First published in 2014 by
Franklin Watts
338 Euston Road
London
NW1 3BH

Franklin Watts Australia
Level 17/207 Kent Street
Sydney
NSW 2000

Text © Margaret Nash 2014
Illustration © Tripee 2014

The rights of Margaret Nash to be
identified as the author and Tripee as the
illustrator of this Work have been asserted in
accordance with the Copyright, Designs and
Patents Act, 1988.

A CIP catalogue record for this book is
available from the British Library.

ISBN 978 1 4451 3218 1 (hbk)
ISBN 978 1 4451 3219 8 (pbk)
ISBN 978 1 4451 3220 4 (ebook)
ISBN 978 1 4451 3221 1 (library ebook)

Series Editor: Jackie Hamley
Editor: Melanie Palmer
Series Advisor: Catherine Glavina
Series Designer: Peter Scoulding

Printed in China

Franklin Watts is a division of Hachette Children's Books,
an Hachette UK company. www.hachette.co.uk